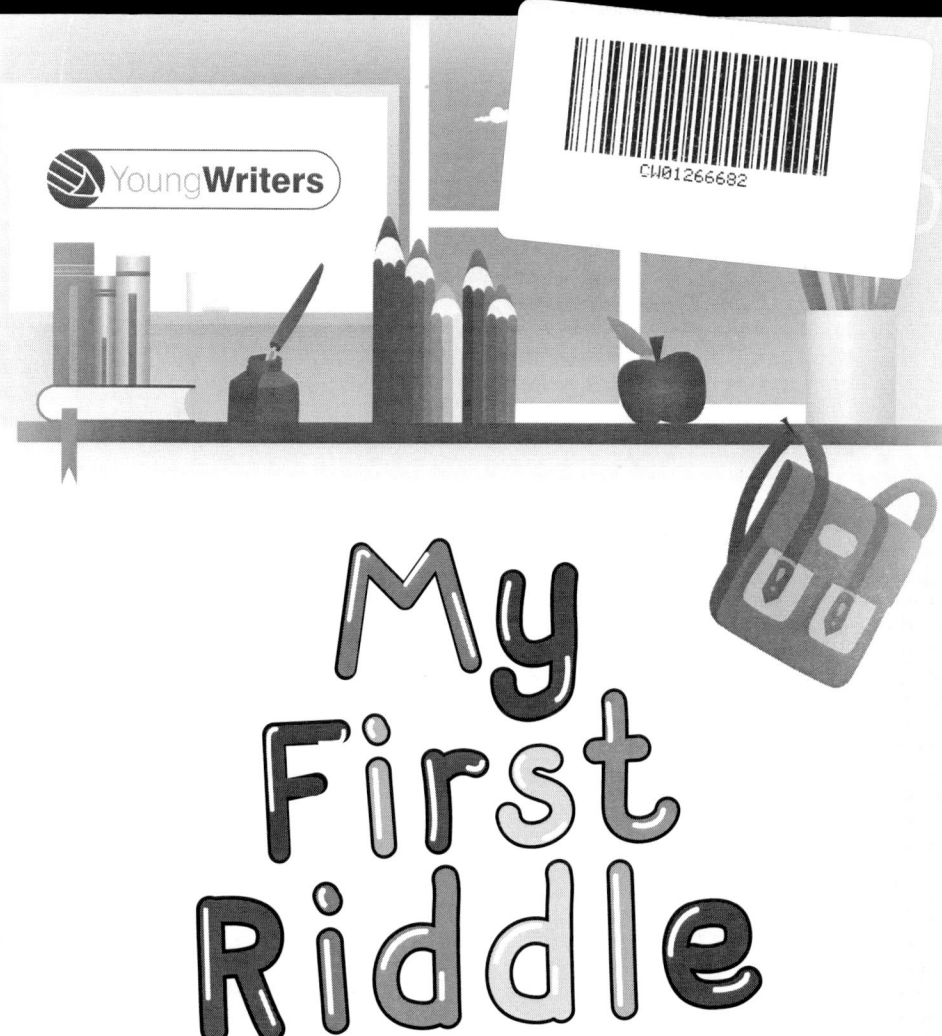

My First Riddle

Little Riddlers

Edited by Helen Davies

First published in Great Britain in 2011 by:
Young Writers

Remus House
Coltsfoot Drive
Peterborough
PE2 9BF
Telephone: 01733 890066
Website: www.youngwriters.co.uk

All Rights Reserved
© Copyright Contributors 2011
SB ISBN 978-0-85739-364-7

Foreword

'My First Riddle' was a competition specifically designed for Key Stage 1 children. The simple, fun form of the riddle gives even the youngest and least confident writers the chance to become interested in poetry by giving them a framework within which to shape their ideas. As well as this it also allows older children to let their creativity flow as much as possible, encouraging the use of simile and descriptive language.

Given the young age of the entrants, we have tried to include as many poems as possible. We believe that seeing their work in print will inspire a love of reading and writing and give these young poets the confidence to develop their skills in the future.

Our defining aim at Young Writers is to foster the talent of the next generation of authors. We are proud to present this latest collection of anthologies and hope you agree that they are an excellent showcase of young writing talent.

Contents

Bargarran Primary School, Erskine

Evie Marshall
& Rachael Hepburn (6) 1
Lewis Steele & Kyle (6) 1
Ciaran, Jonjo
& Robbie Carruthers 2
Lisa, Amy Greenshields
& Rebecca McEwan (6) 2
Eilidh McColl & Caitlin (6) 3
Andrew Whyte & Daniel (6) 3
Dillan & Callum McCrae (6) 4
Carina & Millie Docherty (6) 4

Denny Primary School, Denny

Natalie Wallace (6) 5
Christopher McPake (6) 5
Jay Hall (5) 6
Adam Paterson (6) 6
Rhys Clark (6) 7
Rachel Kerr (6) 7
Lucas Guthrie Allan (7) 8
Jasmine Malik (7) 8
Rhegan Hully (7) 9
Jamie Beattie (7) 9
Mirren Cairns (6) 10
Sandy Binnie (7) 10
Finlay Laird (6) 11
Vicki McFie (7) 11

Evenwood CE Primary School, Evenwood

Caicy Turner (5) 12
Matt Shield (6) 12
Paige Bolingbroke (5) 13
Summer Nicole Geddes (6) 13
Sumayyah Rose Abuelmaatti (5) 14
Hannah Spence (6) 14

Fairfield Park Lower School, Stotfold

Abigail Keddie (5) 15
Hannah Cranston (5) 15
Alice Lacy (5) 16
Nathan Ajibawo (5) 16
Sophie Tiplady (5) 17

Zak Obruk (5) 17
Chantel Straker (5) 18
Thea Pilch (5) 18
Bethan Lily Gerrard (5) 19
Taylor Stevens (5) 19
Sophie Welford (5) 20
Amber Holmes (5) 20
Calum Burton (5) 21
Alessandro Borzellino (5) 21
Rose Ellis Rance (5) 22
Charlotte Caresmel (5) 22
James Charlton (5) 23
Hannah Dewar (5) 23
Molly Constable (6) 24
Daniel Gilchrist (6) 24
Mikey Cary (6) 25
Tillie Armstrong (6) 25
Jacob Ramel (6) 26
Jack Jarrett (6) 26
Rhys McDonald (5) 27
Abby Finka (6) 27
Kyla Li (6) 28
Katie Morton (6) 28
Henry Porter-Robinson (6) 29

Garlieston Primary School, Garlieston

Sam Donkin (6) 29
Callum Hedley (4) 30
Aaron Murray (5) 30
Tom Donkin (5) 31
Sian Ford (7) 31
Sarah Sunderland (7) 32

Green Hammerton Primary School, York

James Harvey (6) 32
Amye Richardson (7) 33
Emma Robeson (5) 33
Luke Temple (6) 34
Olivia Wood (5) 34
Jake Perkins-Hill, Jake Dawson,
Tom Weatherill, William Holloway,
Lola Graham, Jacob Ross
& Ethan Fox (5) 35

Finlay Coad, Lucie Davis,
Ben O'Connor, William Renny,
Hattie Councell
& Cameron Leverton (5) 35
Ethan Knights, Ambur Ashcroft,
Rosie Morrison (5)
& Caleb Graham (6) 36

Greystones Primary School, Sheffield

Daniel Redfearn (5) 36
Sophie Robinson (5) 37
Esther Meakin (6) 37
Tor Bramble (5) 38
Matteo Marshall (5) 38
Amelie Fenton (6) 39
Gracie Faulkner (5) 39
Isobel Dolan (5) 40
Evan Raw (5) 40
Olivia Kirby (5) 41
Ruby Gradwell (5) 41
Harvey Fretwell (5) 42
Haleemah Asif (5) 42
Holly Bonser (5) 43
Eilidh Murray-Stringer (5) 43
Jasper Barnsley (5) 44
Michaela Macreath-Smith (5) 44

Heworth CE Primary School, York

Grace Millard (6) 45
Joshua Dyke (6) 45
Maggie-Jo Allan (6) 46
Jemma Blanchard (6) 46

Hightae Primary School, Hightae

Euan Millar (10) 47
Keir Millar (6) 47
Euan Muirhead (6) 48
Jack Muirhead (8) 48
Casey McConnell (10) 49
Shannon McConnell (8) 49
Harry Chadwick (8) 50
Kibbe Watson (7) 50
Ari Watson (8) 51
Millie Peacock (10) 51
Marnix Vandenhoucke (9) 52
Tamara Brown (10) 52

Angus Collison (11) 53
Joshua Newbould (9) 53
Euan Davidson (10) 54

New Delaval Primary School, Blyth

Aaron Lowe (6) 54
Aaron Freeman (6) 55
Catelyn Osbourne (6) 55
Bobby Rowlandson (6) 56
Chloe Mitchell (6) 56
Teigan Luke (7) 57
Chris Davis (6) 57
Shannon Winter (6) 58
Daneka Murray (6) 58

Rudston Preparatory School, Rotherham

Saoirse Behan (6) 59
Mason Booth (7) 59
Eshaan Chandran (6) 60
Alex Cox (6) 60
Chardonnay Johnstone (6) 61
Mia Jones (6) 61
Tom Lockwood (6) 62
Emily Robinson-Perkins (6) 62
Ankush Sharma (7) 63
Ethan Tattershall-Waller (6) 63
William Tolley (6) 64
Abbeygail Wrennall (7) 64

St Clement's RC Primary School, Dundee

Liam Tugman (7) 65
Callum Valentine (7) 65
Ryan Small (5) 66
Amy Rennie (7) 66
Nadine Ellott (6) 67

St Hilary's Primary School, St Leonard's

Abbie Kirwan (6) 67
Rachel Donnachie (7) 68
Andrew Roxburgh (6) 68
Joseph Finan (6) 69
Alex McGowan (7) 69
Nathan Rattray (6) 70
Issabella Drennan (7) 70
Jenna Villani (6) 71

St Joseph's RC Primary School, Aberdeen

Michael Herrera (6)	71
Ella Megginson (6)	72
Cole Truscott (6)	72
Patrick Rogerson (6)	73
Chloe Scott (7)	73
Summer Avalos (6)	74
Teagan Kelly (6)	74
Josef Bokedal (6)	75
Heather Reid (6)	75
Shane Purcell (6)	76
Aisling McMenemy (7)	76
Deidra Dias Alberto (5)	77
Leah McAllister (6)	77
Cian Mair (6)	78
Ben Scott (5)	78

St Matthew's RC Primary School, Jarrow

Tyler Kelly (6)	79
Sophie Grimes (6)	79
Daniel Stark (6)	80
Alexandra McLeod (6)	80
Emily Bateman (6)	81
Alex James Currie (7)	81
Tom Paterson (6)	82
Libby Robertson (6)	82
Erin Bryce (6)	83
Jack Thomas Gibson (5)	83
Harry Birrell (5)	84
Cain Harry Conner (5)	84
Matthew Sproston (5)	85
Thomas Booth & Jay Robinson (5)	85

St Ninian's Primary School, Dedridge

Niamh Sharkey (5)	86
Chrissy Annal (6)	86
Alan B Shibu (6)	87
Jodie Lee Scott (6)	87
Taylor Green (6)	88
Daniel Strickland (7)	88
Andrew Robertson (7)	89
Katie Meldrum	89
Katie Coyle (7)	90
Meghan McVey (7)	90
Roha Ajmal (7)	91
Euan Scott (6)	91
Dylan Polland	92
Aaron Duddridge (7)	92
Daniel Miller (7)	93
Aliya Iqbal	93
Katherine Robertson (7)	94
Lucy Neilson	94
Rachael McMaster	95
Aimee White	95
Emma Thomson	96
Amy Wood (7)	96

St Robert's RC Primary School, Bridgend

Ioan Borromeo (5)	97
Osian Howell-Doyle (5)	97
Yasmine Evans (5)	98
George Hunt (5)	98
Ewan Bailey (5)	99
Jake Stocks (5)	99
Emily Lloyd (6)	100
Elis James (6)	100
Amelia Rees (6)	101
Elis Major (6)	101
Sophie Hunter (7)	102
Zoe Thomas (6)	102
Cavan Frowen (6)	103
Kitty Long (6)	103
Evan Gregory (6)	104
Orlando Diogo (7)	104
Niamh Harris (6)	105
Ruben Morgan (7)	105
Davide Belsole (6)	106
Chloe Protheroe (6)	106
Owen Stone (6)	107

South Wootton First School, South Wootton

Talisha Cooper (7)	107
Olivia Sharp (7)	108
Caitlin McCallum (6)	108
Cameron Reed (7)	109
Sophie Moyse (6)	109
Harry Ponting (6)	110
Brad Denham (6)	110
Tayah Farnham (7)	111
Chloe McGiven (7)	111

Emily Cullen (6) 112
Sophie Morgan (7) 112
Callum Eke (6) 113

Stanley Grove School, Wakefield

Cody Sharratt (6) 113
Michael Blick (6) 114
Hollie Smith (6) 114
Amelia Ashton (5) 115
Mason Nunn (6) 115
Ellie Wilkinson (6) 116
Caris Riley (6) 116
Amy Whyte (6) 117
Alice Aveyard (5) 117
Abigail Cooney (6) 118
Joseph Berry (6) 118
Georgina Odgers (6) 119
Katie Whyte (6) 119
Ella Crispin (6) 120
Paige Wright (5) 120

Star Of The Sea RC Primary School, Whitley Bay

John Campbell (6) 121
Molly Dutton (6) 121
James May (6) 122
Kian MacOscar (6) 122
Isabel Hines (6) 123
Barbod Farokhzad (7) 123
Jonny Worrall (6) 124
Chrysta Lois (6) 124
Amelia Slaven (6) 125
Chloe-Marie Davison (6) 125
Gabriel Darcy (6) 126
Amy Tullock (6) 126
Joseph Mathew (7) 127
Bella Gott (7) 127
Abigail Stephenson (6)........................ 128
Dominic Dixon (7) 128
Martha Foreman (7) 129
Josephine Perella (6).......................... 129

Tanfield Lea Primary School, Stanley

Drew Lake (6) 130
Anais Little (7) 130
Tia Bailey (7) 131
Elle Stark (6) 131
Jamie Miley (6) 132

Beth Nash (6) 132
Lauren Urquhart-Arnold (6) 133
Aron Alderson (6) 133
Allana Alderson (6)............................. 134
Rebecca Bell (6) 134
Ben Henley (6)..................................... 135
Joe Little (6)... 135
Tamzin McAdam (7) 136
Sophie Steel (6).................................. 136

Tundergarth Primary School, Lockerbie

James Collinge (5) 137
Kelly Halliday (6).................................. 137
Sandy Temple (5) 138
Dari Earl (5) 138

The Poems

My First Riddle – Little Riddlers

What Is It?

As hairy as a cat
As loud as a fire alarm
As tall as a toddler
As heavy as a chair
It's a dog.

Evie Marshall & Rachael Hepburn (6)
Bargarran Primary School, Erskine

What Is It?

It's as cheeky as a monkey
It's as camouflaged as green grass
Its tongue is as long as a giraffe's neck
It's as small as an ant
It's a lizard.

Lewis Steele & Kyle (6)
Bargarran Primary School, Erskine

What Is It?

It's as fast as a treadmill
It can jump like a dolphin
It's as black as night
You can ride it like a roller coaster
It's a horse.

Ciaran, Jonjo & Robbie Carruthers
Bargarran Primary School, Erskine

What Is It?

As lovely as Cheryl Cole
As blue and pink as a rainbow
As beautiful as a butterfly
A unicorn.

Lisa, Amy Greenshields & Rebecca McEwan (6)
Bargarran Primary School, Erskine

My First Riddle - Little Riddlers

What Is It?

As fun as the park
As naughty as a monkey
As furry as a kitten
As loud as a horn
It's a dog.

Eilidh McColl & Caitlin (6)
Bargarran Primary School, Erskine

What Is It?

As playful as a puppy
A roar as loud as a motorbike
As big as a car
A tail as long as an elephant's trunk
It's a tiger.

Andrew Whyte & Daniel (6)
Bargarran Primary School, Erskine

What Is It?

Its tongue is as long as a giraffe.
It can run as fast as a cheetah.
It can climb trees like a monkey.
It is small like an ant.

It is a lizard.

Dillan & Callum McCrae (6)
Bargarran Primary School, Erskine

What Is It?

It's as furry as a feather.
It's as cute as a baby.
It's as fast as a bike.
It's as cheeky as a monkey.
It's a cat.

Carina & Millie Docherty (6)
Bargarran Primary School, Erskine

My First Riddle - Little Riddlers

My Dog, Holly

She's as small as a handbag.
She's as naughty as a monkey.
She's as noisy as a trumpet.
She's as cuddly as a cat.
She is my dog, Holly.

Natalie Wallace (6)
Denny Primary School, Denny

Untitled

He's as funny as a clown
He's as handsome as Prince Charming
He's as cool as a cucumber.
He is my dad.

Christopher McPake (6)
Denny Primary School, Denny

My Mum

She's as funny as a clown.
She's as good as gold.
She's as busy as a bee.
She is my mum.

Jay Hall (5)
Denny Primary School, Denny

Iron Man

He is as strong as steel
And as fast as lightning
His suit is as red as a postbox
His suit is as hard as a rock
He is Iron Man.

Adam Paterson (6)
Denny Primary School, Denny

My First Riddle - Little Riddlers

My Friend

He is as fast as roller skates
He is as funny as a clown
He is as nice as a koala bear
He is as fluffy as a cloud
He is as kind as a king
He is my friend, Kyle.

Rhys Clark (6)
Denny Primary School, Denny

My Friend

She is as fast as a mouse.
She is as big as a gorilla.
She is as beautiful as a flower.
She is as funny as a monkey.
She is as cuddly as a rabbit.
She is my friend, Megan.

Rachel Kerr (6)
Denny Primary School, Denny

My Friend

He is as cool as a koala.
He is as fast as a racing car.
He is fantastic at his work.
He is as good as gold.
He is as funny as a clown.
He is as amazing as an acrobat.
His name is Sandy Binnie.

Lucas Guthrie Allan (7)
Denny Primary School, Denny

My Friend

She is as big as a rock star.
She is as amazing as a star.
She is as helpful as a girl.
She is as fast as a racer.
She is as lovely as a flower.
She is my friend, Ellie.

Jasmine Malik (7)
Denny Primary School, Denny

My First Riddle - Little Riddlers

My Friend

He is as cool as a teacher.
He is as fast as a bullet.
He is as dangerous as a shark.
He is as fantastic as a rock star.
He is as bad as a monkey.
He is my friend, Finlay.

Rhegan Hully (7)
Denny Primary School, Denny

My Friend

He is as fast as a bullet.
He is as funny as a clown.
He is as sweet as apples.
He is as cool as a monkey.
He is my friend, Finlay.

Jamie Beattie (7)
Denny Primary School, Denny

My Friend

She is as cool as a dolphin.
She is as funny as a clown.
She is as lovely as a princess.
She is as fast as a cheetah.
She is as super as a superhero.
She is my friend, Katie.

Mirren Cairns (6)
Denny Primary School, Denny

My Friend

He is as smart as a teacher.
He is as cheeky as a monkey.
He is as funny as a clown.
He is as cool as a rock star.
He is as skinny as a mouse.
He is my friend, Keigan.

Sandy Binnie (6)
Denny Primary School, Denny

My First Riddle - Little Riddlers

My Friend

He is as smart as a gorilla.
He is as cool as a king.
He is as cold as an ice cream.
He is as fantastic as a cheetah.
He is as funny as a clown.
He is called Jamie.

Finlay Laird (6)
Denny Primary School, Denny

My Friend

She is as lovely as a flower
She is as fast as a cheetah
She is as good as gold
She is as funny as a clown
She is as cheeky as a monkey
She is my friend, Becky.

Vicki McFie (7)
Denny Primary School, Denny

What Is It?

It is as long as a snake
It whistles like a kettle
It is as shiny as the sun

It is a train.

Caicy Turner (5)
Evenwood CE Primary School, Evenwood

What Is It?

It is as fast as a cheetah.
It is as dirty as mud.
It is as noisy as an elephant.

It is a motorbike.

Matt Shield (6)
Evenwood CE Primary School, Evenwood

My First Riddle - Little Riddlers

What Is It?

It is as bumpy as a ride.
It is faster than a car.
It is as light as a feather.
It has one eye like an alien.

It is a motorbike.

Paige Bolingbroke (5)
Evenwood CE Primary School, Evenwood

What Is It?

It is as fast as a gorilla
It is as noisy as a sheep
It is as shiny as money
It is prettier than a kid

It is a car.

Summer Nicole Geddes (6)
Evenwood CE Primary School, Evenwood

What Is It?

It is as fast as a leopard
It is as long as a crocodile
It moves from side to side like a crab

It is a train.

Sumayyah Rose Abuelmaatti (5)
Evenwood CE Primary School, Evenwood

What Is It?

It is as big as a tree.
It is smaller than a giant.
It is as fat as a cow.

It is a jeep.

Hannah Spence (6)
Evenwood CE Primary School, Evenwood

My First Riddle - Little Riddlers

What Am I?

I am crunchy.
I am green and red.
I am juicy and I am shiny.
I am a sphere.
What am I?

I am an apple.

Abigail Keddie (5)
Fairfield Park Lower School, Stotfold

What Am I?

I have seeds.
I am soft.
I am juicy.
I am red.
What am I?

I am a tomato.

Hannah Cranston (5)
Fairfield Park Lower School, Stotfold

What Am I?

I am crunchy
I am hard
I have pips
I like them
What am I?

I am an apple.

Alice Lacy (5)
Fairfield Park Lower School, Stotfold

What Am I?

I am hard
I am crunchy
I am long
I am orange
What am I?

I am a carrot.

Nathan Ajibawo (5)
Fairfield Park Lower School, Stotfold

My First Riddle – Little Riddlers

What Am I?

I am hard.
I am crunchy.
I am round.
I grow from a tree.
What am I?

I am an apple.

Sophie Tiplady (5)
Fairfield Park Lower School, Stotfold

What Am I?

I am hairy
I am round
I am brown
I am green
What am I?

I am a kiwi.

Zak Obruk (5)
Fairfield Park Lower School, Stotfold

What Am I?

I am hard.
I am crunchy.
I have skin.
What am I?

I am an apple.

Chantel Straker (5)
Fairfield Park Lower School, Stotfold

What Am I?

I am crunchy
I am hard
I am bumpy
I am juicy
I am hairy
I am long
What am I?

I am a carrot.

Thea Pilch (5)
Fairfield Park Lower School, Stotfold

What Am I?

I am crunchy
I am hard
I am juicy
I am green
I have pips in
What am I?

I am an apple.

Bethan Lily Gerrard (5)
Fairfield Park Lower School, Stotfold

What Am I?

I am soft
I have skin.
I am yellow.
I am bent.
What am I?

A banana.

Taylor Stevens (5)
Fairfield Park Lower School, Stotfold

What Am I?

I am juicy
I am sweet
I am round
I am green when I am not ripe
I am red
What am I?

I am a tomato.

Sophie Welford (5)
Fairfield Park Lower School, Stotfold

What Am I?

I am juicy
I am hairy
I am round
I am sweet
What am I?

I am a kiwi.

Amber Holmes (5)
Fairfield Park Lower School, Stotfold

My First Riddle - Little Riddlers

What Am I?

I am smooth
I am round
I am crunchy
What am I?

I am an apple.

Calum Burton (5)
Fairfield Park Lower School, Stotfold

What Am I?

I am yellow
I am curved
I am soft
What am I?

I am a banana.

Alessandro Borzellino (5)
Fairfield Park Lower School, Stotfold

What Am I?

I have a green bit at the top
I am soft
I have seeds
I am red
I am round
I am smooth
I am juicy
What am I?

I am a tomato.

Rose Ellis Rance (5)
Fairfield Park Lower School, Stotfold

What Am I?

I am juicy
I have pips
I am crunchy
I am green
I am round
What am I?

I am an apple.

Charlotte Caresmel (5)
Fairfield Park Lower School, Stotfold

My First Riddle – Little Riddlers

What Am I?

I am soft
I have pips
I am yellow
What am I?

A lemon.

James Charlton (5)
Fairfield Park Lower School, Stotfold

What Am I?

I am crunchy
I am hairy
I am long
I am bumpy
What am I?

I am a carrot.

Hannah Dewar (5)
Fairfield Park Lower School, Stotfold

What Am I?

I am orange
I am juicy
I am red
You can pick me
What am I?

I am an apple.

Molly Constable (6)
Fairfield Park Lower School, Stotfold

What Am I?

I am red and green.
I am sweet.
I am healthy.
What am I?

I am a watermelon.

Daniel Gilchrist (6)
Fairfield Park Lower School, Stotfold

My First Riddle - Little Riddlers

What Am I?

I am yellow,
I am spiky,
I have a stalk,
I need to be cut to be eaten,
I am juicy,
I have black seeds,
I grow on trees,
I don't grow in the ground,
What am I?

I am a pineapple.

Mikey Cary (6)
Fairfield Park Lower School, Stotfold

What Am I?

I am juicy.
I am round.
I can be cooked.
I can be raw.
I am squashy.
I have pips.
I am healthy.
What am I?

I am a tomato.

Tillie Armstrong (6)
Fairfield Park Lower School, Stotfold

What Am I?

I am round and juicy.
I am red and green.
I grow on trees.
I am soft and have black seeds.
What am I?

I am an apple.

Jacob Ramel (6)
Fairfield Park Lower School, Stotfold

What Am I?

I grow on a tree
I am red
I am small
I am shiny
I have a stone
I have a stalk
I am round
What am I?

I am a cherry.

Jack Jarrett (6)
Fairfield Park Lower School, Stotfold

My First Riddle - Little Riddlers

What Am I?

I am red
I have pips
I am squashy
I am yellow inside
I am round
What am I?

I am a plum.

Rhys McDonald (5)
Fairfield Park Lower School, Stotfold

What Am I?

I am sour
I have tiny pips
I am smooth
I grow on trees
I have extremely tough skin
I can be squeezed
I am juicy and tangy
What am I?

I am a lemon.

Abby Finka (6)
Fairfield Park Lower School, Stotfold

What Am I?

I am orange
I am round
I sometimes have pips
I am soft
I am juicy
I am squashy
What am I?

I am an orange.

Kyla Li (6)
Fairfield Park Lower School, Stotfold

What Am I?

I am red
I am round
I have a stalk
I grow on trees
I am shiny
I have seeds inside me
I am healthy
I am scrummy
I am yummy
What am I?

I am an apple.

Katie Morton (6)
Fairfield Park Lower School, Stotfold

My First Riddle - Little Riddlers

What Am I?

I am orange
I am juicy
I am tangy
I am tasty
What am I?

I am an orange.

Henry Porter-Robinson (6)
Fairfield Park Lower School, Stotfold

Halloween Riddle

He is as bad as a robot.
He is as ugly as a frog.
He is as scary as a giant spider.
He is a dead man.
He is a zombie.

Sam Donkin (6)
Garlieston Primary School, Garlieston

Halloween Riddle

He drives a van as fast as a quadbike,
He catches ghosts as fast as a motorbike,
He is as good as a cat,
He is a ghostbuster.

Callum Hedley (4)
Garlieston Primary School, Garlieston

Transformer Riddle

He's as big as the tallest tower,
He's as good as a robot,
He's as fast as a motorbike,
He is Optimus Prime.

Aaron Murray (5)
Garlieston Primary School, Garlieston

Halloween Riddle

Its fangs are as sharp as a knife,
Its legs are as long as a bat,
It has spots like a Dalmatian,
It's a spider.

Tom Donkin (5)
Garlieston Primary School, Garlieston

Halloween Riddle

She's as bad as a bumblebee.
She's as ugly as a shark.
She's as nasty as a jellyfish.
Her hair is as long as a bear.
She's as stinky as a toad.
She is a witch.

Sian Ford (7)
Garlieston Primary School, Garlieston

Halloween Riddle

He's as tall as the Empire State Building.
He's as ugly as a wart.
He's as strong as an elephant.
He's bleeding like a bad cut.
He's as scary as a witch.
He's Frankenstein.

Sarah Sunderland (7)
Garlieston Primary School, Garlieston

Who Am I?

He is as strong as Superman
He is as old as my mum
He is as big as a giant
He is as bold as the world
He is as clever as Mr Clever!
He is my dad.

James Harvey (6)
Green Hammerton Primary School, York

My First Riddle - Little Riddlers

Who Am I?

She is as pretty as Mrs Sanderson
She is as nice as a guinea pig
She is a fantastic singer like me
She is as popular as a princess
She has hair as brown as bark on a tree
She is Miley Cyrus.

Amye Richardson (7)
Green Hammerton Primary School, York

Who Am I?

She is pretty like a kitten
She is colourful like a rainbow
She is famous like Christopher Wilds
She sings like a bird
She is Hannah Montana.

Emma Robeson (5)
Green Hammerton Primary School, York

Who Am I?

He is as fast as a cheetah
He is wearing white like snow
He is as quiet as a mouse
He is The Stig.

Luke Temple (6)
Green Hammerton Primary School, York

Who Am I?

She is as pretty as a flower
She can sing like an angel
She is as bright as the sun
She is Hannah Montana.

Olivia Wood (5)
Green Hammerton Primary School, York

My First Riddle – Little Riddlers

Who Am I?

She is as cheeky as a monkey.
She is happy as can be.
Her lips are as pink as roses.
She is exciting like a volcano.
She is Mrs Metcalfe.

Jake Perkins-Hill, Jake Dawson, Tom Weatherill, William Holloway, Lola Graham, Jacob Ross & Ethan Fox (5)
Green Hammerton Primary School, York

Who Am I?

He is as happy as a clown
He is kind like my mummy
He is as jolly as can be
He is cuddly like my teddy
His coat is as red as a berry
He is Father Christmas.

Finlay Coad, Lucie Davis, Ben O'Connor, William Renny, Hattie Councell & Cameron Leverton (5)
Green Hammerton Primary School, York

Who Am I?

She is as kind as our teacher, Mrs Sanderson
She is in charge like the Queen or government
She is helpful like the police
She is beautiful like a rose
She is lovable like my pets
She is caring like a mummy
She is as funny as a clown
She is Mrs Wallis, our head teacher.

Ethan Knights, Ambur Ashcroft, Rosie Morrison (5) & Caleb Graham (6)
Green Hammerton Primary School, York

Who Is It?

Its eyes are as big as a hula hoop
Its tail is bushier than a squirrel
It lives in a tree
It is as cuddly as a teddy

. . . it is a bush baby.

Daniel Redfearn (5)
Greystones Primary School, Sheffield

My First Riddle - Little Riddlers

Who Is It?

Its tail is as long as a snake
It's as furry as a pillow
It's as fast as an ant
It lives under the floorboards

. . . it is a mouse.

Sophie Robinson (5)
Greystones Primary School, Sheffield

Who Am I?

I am as cuddly as a cuddly toy
I am as orange as a fox
My purr is as loud as a motorbike
My ears are as sharp as needles

I am a . . . cat.

Esther Meakin (6)
Greystones Primary School, Sheffield

Who Am I?

I am as spotty as a ladybird
I am as quiet as a mouse
I am as soft as a teddy

I am a leopard.

Tor Bramble (5)
Greystones Primary School, Sheffield

Who Am I?

I am as fast as a racing car
I am as black as a school jumper
I can fly as high as a rocket

I am a . . . bat.

Matteo Marshall (5)
Greystones Primary School, Sheffield

My First Riddle - Little Riddlers

Who Am I?

I am as cuddly as a teddy
I am as fluffy as cotton wool
I am as orange as a fox
I am better than a mouse trap
I am as gentle as a dog

I am a cat.

Amelie Fenton (6)
Greystones Primary School, Sheffield

Who Am I?

I am as soft as a feather.
I am as black as a cardigan.
My ears are as floppy as an elephant
My bark is as loud as a horn

I am a dog.

Gracie Faulkner (5)
Greystones Primary School, Sheffield

Who Am I?

I am as soft as a feather
I am as brown as a bear
My ears are as pointy as a triangle
I am as loud as a rocket
I eat apples

I am a horse.

Isobel Dolan (5)
Greystones Primary School, Sheffield

Who Is It?

Its poison is as sharp as a wasp sting
It's got lots of legs like a spider
It lives in the sea like a sea snail
It is as wobbly as a jelly

It is a . . . jellyfish.

Evan Raw (5)
Greystones Primary School, Sheffield

My First Riddle – Little Riddlers

Who Is It?

It is as soft as a teddy
It is as small as a mouse
It likes to bite apple sticks
It runs in a wheel in its cage

It is a . . . hamster.

Olivia Kirby (5)
Greystones Primary School, Sheffield

Animal Riddle

It is as cuddly as a teddy bear
It is as floppy as a doggy's ears
It is as bouncy as a bouncy ball
It is as black as a bear
It is as white as a polar bear
It is a rabbit.

Ruby Gradwell (5)
Greystones Primary School, Sheffield

Animal Riddle

It is as dangerous as a shark
It is as scaly as a lizard
It is as fast as the wind
It is as poisonous as anything
It is a komodo dragon.

Harvey Fretwell (5)
Greystones Primary School, Sheffield

Animal Riddle

It is as cute as a squirrel
It is as sleepy as a baby
It is as floppy as a hand
It is as kind as a person
It is a rabbit.

Haleemah Asif (5)
Greystones Primary School, Sheffield

My First Riddle - Little Riddlers

What Am I?

I am as fast as the wind
I am stripy like jim jams,
Black and white like a crossing,
Proud, beautiful and cute.
I am a zebra.

Holly Bonser (5)
Greystones Primary School, Sheffield

Animal Riddle

It is as cute as a cat
It is as soft as a blanket
It is as slow as a hedgehog
It is as scared as a mouse
It is as hungry as a horse
It is a guinea pig.

Eilidh Murray-Stringer (5)
Greystones Primary School, Sheffield

Animal Riddle

It is as fierce as a shark
It is as clever as a bush baby
It is as fast as a car
It is an owl.

Jasper Barnsley (5)
Greystones Primary School, Sheffield

Animal Riddle

It is as furry as a lion
It is kinder than a hamster
It is gentler than a rabbit
It is softer than a guinea pig
It is beautiful
It is a horse.

Michaela Macreath-Smith (5)
Greystones Primary School, Sheffield

My First Riddle - Little Riddlers

What Am I?

I'm very loud
I make a funny sound
I'm golden and sparkly
I have buttons on me
I play in a band
You can't eat me.

What am I . . . ?

I'm a trumpet.

Grace Millard (6)
Heworth CE Primary School, York

What Am I?

I am scaly
I slither around on the ground
I live in the jungle
I slither up trees
I sleep in a coil
I have a y-shaped tongue
I shed my skin off on a tree
What am I?
I am a snake.

Joshua Dyke (6)
Heworth CE Primary School, York

What Am I?

I have fire in me.
I blow up.
I go into the air.
I fly away.
I have rope on me.
I am colourful.
You cannot hear me.
What am I?
I am a hot air balloon.

Maggie-Jo Allan (6)
Heworth CE Primary School, York

What Am I?

I have hair around my head
I can't run like a leopard
I'm asleep a lot
I go roar!
My head is scary
What am I?
I am a lion.

Jemma Blanchard (6)
Heworth CE Primary School, York

My Air Rifle

It is as patterned as a picture,
It has as much concentration needed as a sniper rifle,
It is as brown as a piece of wood,
It is as heavy as a full paper bin,
It is as hard to break as a tree,
It is as smooth as a sheet of paper,
It is as old as our house,
It is my air rifle.

Euan Millar (10)
Hightae Primary School, Hightae

Harry

He is as funny as a clown
He is as good as a mum
He is as cool as a tiger
He is as brown as a deer
He is as arty as the art teacher
He is as young as a dad
He is as selfish as a monkey
He is like a human being
He is Harry.

Keir Millar (6)
Hightae Primary School, Hightae

My Monkey

He is as cheeky as a clown
He is as lively as a human,
He is as furry as a poodle,
He is as fast as a rocket,
He is as smooth as a dog,
He is as hairy as a lion,
He can climb like a gorilla,
He is as bad as a robber,
He is as brown as a tree trunk,
He is a monkey.

Euan Muirhead (6)
Hightae Primary School, Hightae

My Dog, Bo

He is as loyal as a mum,
He is as fragile as glass,
He is as fun as a ball,
He is as springy as a rabbit,
He is as noisy as a horn,
He is as pleasant as a friend,
He is as fast as a rocket,
He is as warm as a bowl of soup,
He is as wiry as hair,
He is my dog, Bo.

Jack Muirhead (8)
Hightae Primary School, Hightae

Hannah Montana

She is as beautiful as the queen,
She is as funny as a monkey,
She is a superstar,
She can sing and dance,
She is Hannah Montana.

Casey McConnell (10)
Hightae Primary School, Hightae

Keir

He is as silly as a monkey,
He is as noisy as a helicopter,
He is as cool as a rock band,
He is as funny as a joker,
He is as small as Harry,
He is as arty as an artist,
He is as gentle as a rabbit,
He has brown hair like a deer,
He is as fun as a swing park,
He is as active as a builder,
He is as annoying as a sister,
He is as naughty as a chimpanzee,
He is as cheerful as a mum,
He is as fast as a car,
He is Keir.

Shannon McConnell (8)
Hightae Primary School, Hightae

My Dogtag

It is as light as a feather,
It is as delicate as a tissue,
It is as special as a cat,
It is as rattly as a bell,
It is as hard as a brick,
It is as old as a horse,
It is as little as a strip of paper,
It is as silver as a mirror.

Harry Chadwick (8)
Hightae Primary School, Hightae

My Cat

She is as cute as a robin,
She likes to play with my finger,
She is as nice as my sister,
She is as light as a toy mouse,
She is as funny as a monkey,
She is my cat.

Kibbe Watson (7)
Hightae Primary School, Hightae

My Kitten, Rolo

He is as cuddly as a teddy bear,
He is as silly as a monkey,
He is as light as a feather,
He is as small as a box,
He is as fluffy as a cloud,
He is as friendly as me,
He is as loving as a caring person,
He is as funny as a clown,
He is my kitten, Rolo.

Ari Watson (8)
Hightae Primary School, Hightae

My Mum

She is as fun as a roller coaster
She's as enjoyable as an ice cream
She's as lovely as a flower
She's as kind as an angel
She's as helpful as a teacher
She's as generous as a person working in a charity shop
She is my mum.

Millie Peacock (10)
Hightae Primary School, Hightae

My Bike

It's as oily as a 2 litre puddle,
It's as fit as a bear climbing the Mont Blanc,
It's as strong as a big, black, mad bull,
It's as shiny as a diamond,
It's as fast as a gorilla swinging through the trees,
It's as squeaky as a mouse,
It's my bike.

Marnix Vandenhoucke (9)
Hightae Primary School, Hightae

My Necklace

It is as fragile as glass,
It is as bumpy as the bark on a tree,
It is as shiny as silver,
It is as old as my dead friend,
It is as precious as my family,
It is as memorable as the Second World War,
It is as twinkly as the stars,
It is as smooth as melted chocolate,
It is as white as white sugar,
It is as long as a ruler,
It is as hard as a tiny rock,
It's my necklace that my friend Pippi gave me.

Tamara Brown (10)
Hightae Primary School, Hightae

My Jet

It is as brittle as a ruler,
It is as challenging as a day at school,
It is as small as a tennis ball,
It is as rough as sand paper,
It is as white as a blank piece of paper,
It is as black as the night sky,
It is as light as a feather,
It is as old as my school jumper,
It is as fragile as some Lego,
It is as shiny as a crystal,
It is my Model Mirage F1.

Angus Collison (11)
Hightae Primary School, Hightae

Yogi My Cat

He is as selfish as a king,
He is as bold as a policeman,
He is as funny as a clown,
He is as greedy as a lion,
He is as fast as a cheetah,
He is as playful as a friend,
He is as young as a baby,
He is as fluffy as a rabbit,
He is as brown as wood,
He is Yogi, my cat.

Joshua Newbould (9)
Hightae Primary School, Hightae

My Medal

It is as smooth as silk,
It is as special as the sun,
It is as round as a ball,
It is as hard as a rock,
It is as light as a grain of salt,
It is as new as a baby,
It is as important as oxygen,
It is my medal.

Euan Davidson (10)
Hightae Primary School, Hightae

Racing Car

I am very fast like Eurostar
I am as noisy as thunder
I glide like a plane around the track
My laps are timed
I have big wheels of rubber
Petrol feeds me
Companies put their name on me
I am a racing car.

Aaron Lowe (6)
New Delaval Primary School, Blyth

Rooney

He is as famous as the Queen.
He is as fast as a cheetah.
He is as cool as a cat.
He is the best footballer.
He is Rooney.

Aaron Freeman (6)
New Delaval Primary School, Blyth

Kitten

It is as black as a black bird.
It is as tiny as a chick.
It has sharp teeth.
It makes a noise like this, *miaow!*
It is a kitten.

Catelyn Osbourne (6)
New Delaval Primary School, Blyth

Dog

It is as hairy as a cat.
It has four legs.
It comes in different sizes.
It chases a ball.
It eats meat.
It barks.
It is a dog.

Bobby Rowlandson (6)
New Delaval Primary School, Blyth

Butterfly

I eat nectar
I have six legs
I fly
I used to be a caterpillar
I am a butterfly.

Chloe Mitchell (6)
New Delaval Primary School, Blyth

My First Riddle - Little Riddlers

Rose

It's as gorgeous as a princess
It's as red as a ruby
It smells like perfume
It's as soft as silk
It lives in a bed
It's a rose.

Teigan Luke (7)
New Delaval Primary School, Blyth

Snail

It is as delicate as glass
It is as small as a conker
It is as slow as a tortoise
It is as slimy as a slug
It has a shell for a home
It is a snail.

Chris Davis (6)
New Delaval Primary School, Blyth

Unicorn

It's as beautiful as a kitten
It flies
It has a horn
It is a unicorn.

Shannon Winter (6)
New Delaval Primary School, Blyth

Kitten

It's as soft as a chick
It's as cute as a baby
It's as fluffy as a bunny's tail
It purrs
It is a kitten.

Daneka Murray (6)
New Delaval Primary School, Blyth

My First Riddle - Little Riddlers

Who Can It Be?

He's got a wet nose
He's as fluffy as a teddy
He's got black fur like soot
He's got brown eyes like chocolate
He's as lively as a cheetah
He's got a waggy tail like a cat
He's got lovely bones like biscuits
He's my dog, Billy.

Saoirse Behan (6)
Rudston Preparatory School, Rotherham

What Can It Be?

It is as cheeky as a baboon
It is as playful as a boy
It likes banana to eat
It is as fluffy as a gorilla
It is as annoying as a cat
It is a monkey.

Mason Booth (7)
Rudston Preparatory School, Rotherham

Guess Who?

He has good defence like a lion
He is a footballer
He runs fast like a cheetah
He is a good player
He likes football
He plays for Liverpool Football Club
He plays for England as well
He has blondy-brown hair
He is Steven Gerrard.

Eshaan Chandran (6)
Rudston Preparatory School, Rotherham

Who Can It Be?

He is a cool and funny kid
He has got a friend called James
He is as funny as anything
He rules like a skateboarder
Tom is my best friend.

Alex Cox (6)
Rudston Preparatory School, Rotherham

My First Riddle - Little Riddlers

Untitled

She is more precious than a treasure chest.
She has shiny twitchy ears like a cat.
She has shiny smooth fur.
She has got a wonderful wet nose.
She has got a lovely smile.
She has very shiny eyes.
She is very cute.
And she is Molly my dog.

Chardonnay Johnstone (6)
Rudston Preparatory School, Rotherham

Who Can It Be?

It's a girl
She is famous
She sings 'Round and Round'
She is as stunning as a shimmering, shooting star
She does some lovable acting in Wizards of Waverly Place
She has very special perfume to wear
Her name is Selena Gomez.

Mia Jones (6)
Rudston Preparatory School, Rotherham

Who Can It Be?

He is as playful as a cat.
He is as cuddly as a pile of wool.
He is kind like Emily.
He has green eyes.
He has black and white fur.

Tom Lockwood (6)
Rudston Preparatory School, Rotherham

Who Can They Be?

They are fluffy and cute
They have green eyes and ears that are down
One is black and the other one is brown
They are my rabbits Fudge and Bobbit.

Emily Robinson-Perkins (6)
Rudston Preparatory School, Rotherham

My First Riddle - Little Riddlers

What Can It Be?

Little like a pea
Many colours like a rainbow
Feels soft like a feather
Little tail swaying like a flag
Jumps underwater fast
He is my fish.

Ankush Sharma (7)
Rudston Preparatory School, Rotherham

Who Can It Be?

He is as cheeky as a monkey
He is as nice as a butterfly
He is as loveable as Mrs Horner
He is as smashing as Mason
He is Harrison and he is my brother.

Ethan Tattershall-Waller (6)
Rudston Preparatory School, Rotherham

Who Can It Be?

He is a good shooter
He is the best attack
He is really good at defence
He is Peter Crouch.

William Tolley (6)
Rudston Preparatory School, Rotherham

Who Can It Be?

She is playful and she digs my garden up.
She is the biggest and the best.
She is not harmful.
She is called Tammy.
She is my Old English Sheepdog.

Abbeygail Wrennall (7)
Rudston Preparatory School, Rotherham

My First Riddle - Little Riddlers

Guess What He Is

He is cool like a koala.
He is smart like Miss Lucas.
He is big like a T-rex.
He is gummy like a granny.
He is good like me.
He is great like a helper.
He is a blue whale.

Liam Tugman (7)
St Clement's RC Primary School, Dundee

Guess What He Is

He is fat like a chicken
He is fast like a fox
He is cheeky like a snake
He is good like a duck
He is sweet like a hedgehog
He is a lemur.

Callum Valentine (7)
St Clement's RC Primary School, Dundee

Untitled

He is cute like a puppy
He is small like an ant
He is fierce like a cat
He is cool like a shark
He is wet like rain
He is white like a polar bear
He is a dog.

Ryan Small (5)
St Clement's RC Primary School, Dundee

Guess What She Is

She is fast like a tiger
She is small like a kitten
She is pretty like Miss Lucas
She is cuddly like a teddy bear
She is spotty like my socks
She is fluffy like a chick
She is a cheetah.

Amy Rennie (7)
St Clement's RC Primary School, Dundee

Guess What She Is

She is cool like my sister
She is small like a mouse
She is cute like a puppy
She is cool like me
She is cuddly like a polar bear
She is a cat.

Nadine Ellott (6)
St Clement's RC Primary School, Dundee

Mr T-Rex

He is as big as a school
He is as scary as a tiger
He is as fast as a squirrel
He is as hungry as a horse.

Abbie Kirwan (6)
St Hilary's Primary School, St Leonard's

The Puppy

He is as cute as a ladybird.
He is as playful as a best friend.
His nose is as shiny as glass.
His tongue is as pink as a pig.
His waggy tail is as waggy as a worm.
He is my puppy.

Rachel Donnachie (7)
St Hilary's Primary School, St Leonard's

The Puppy

He is as cute as a cuddly toy.
He is as playful as a hamster.
His nose is as black as a torch.
His tongue is as pink as a pig.
His tail is waggy like a worm.
He is Pete the puppy.

Andrew Roxburgh (6)
St Hilary's Primary School, St Leonard's

Cutie

He is as cute as a cat.
He is as playful as a park.
His nose is as black as my shoe.
His tongue is as long as a pin.
His tail is as waggy as a storm.

Joseph Finan (6)
St Hilary's Primary School, St Leonard's

Untitled

He is as cute as a cat.
He is as playful as toys.
His nose is as black as the night sky.
His tongue is as pink as the pink panther.
His tail is as waggly as a worm.
He is Pete the puppy.

Alex McGowan (7)
St Hilary's Primary School, St Leonard's

Pete The Puppy

He is as cute as a teddy.
He is as playful as a friend.
His nose is as black and shiny as a trophy.
His tongue is as pink as a pig.
His tail is as waggly as a worm.
He is Pete the puppy.

Nathan Rattray (6)
St Hilary's Primary School, St Leonard's

The Butterfly

It is as beautiful as a daisy.
It is as light as a pillow.
It is as small as a baby's hand.
It is as colourful as dots.
It is as wonderful as a Baby Born.
It is as butterfly.

Issabella Drennan (7)
St Hilary's Primary School, St Leonard's

Mr T-Rex

He is as big as a school.
He is as big as a cloud.
He is as big as a double decker.
He is as big as a tree.
He is as big as the world.

Jenna Villani (6)
St Hilary's Primary School, St Leonard's

Cheetah

It is as strong as a rhinoceros,
It is brave like a lion,
It is as big as a tiger,
It is as spotty as a leopard,
It is a cheetah.

Michael Herrera (6)
St Joseph's RC Primary School, Aberdeen

Guinea Pigs

They are as nibbly as a rabbit,
They are as furry as a dog,
They are as squeaky as a mouse,
They are as fast as a leopard,
They are as fat as an elephant,
They are my guinea pigs.

Ella Megginson (6)
St Joseph's RC Primary School, Aberdeen

Fernando Torres

He is as cool as an ice lolly
He is as fast as a fish
He is as fit as a whale
He scores some great goals
He is Fernando Torres.

Cole Truscott (6)
St Joseph's RC Primary School, Aberdeen

My First Riddle - Little Riddlers

Peter From Narnia

He is as strong as a wrestler
He has a sword like a razor
He is a knight who wears medals
He has a shield carved out of metal
He is brave like a king
He is Peter from Narnia.

Patrick Rogerson (6)
St Joseph's RC Primary School, Aberdeen

Cheryl Cole

She is as pretty as a rose
She is as cool as lemonade
She sings like a nightingale
She is as nice as a pie
She has hair that is shiny like the sun
She is Cheryl Cole.

Chloe Scott (7)
St Joseph's RC Primary School, Aberdeen

Tinkerbell

She is as tiny as a bee,
She can fly like a butterfly,
She is as nice as pig,
She is funny like a cat,
She is green like a frog,
She is as happy as a caterpillar,
She is Tinkerbell.

Summer Avalos (6)
St Joseph's RC Primary School, Aberdeen

Hannah Montana

She is pretty like a flower,
She is cool like a cat,
She is funny like a clown,
She sings like an angel,
She is blonde like me,
She is Hannah Montana.

Teagan Kelly (6)
St Joseph's RC Primary School, Aberdeen

My First Riddle – Little Riddlers

Zebras

They are as stripy as a bee,
They are as white as a skeleton,
They are as black as a raven,
They are as fast as a tiger,
They are as furry as a gorilla,
They are zebras.

Josef Bokedal (6)
St Joseph's RC Primary School, Aberdeen

My Sister

She is as kind as a flower,
She is as pretty as a butterfly,
She is as funny as a clown,
She is as fun as a cat,
She is as clever as a rat,
She is my sister.

Heather Reid (6)
St Joseph's RC Primary School, Aberdeen

Steve Backshall

He is brave like a cheetah,
He is as gentle as a mouse,
He is as funny as a clown,
He is as strong as a bull,
He is Steve Backshall from 'Live and Deadly'.

Shane Purcell (6)
St Joseph's RC Primary School, Aberdeen

Princess Fiona

She is as mucky as a pig
She is as funny as a clown
She is as friendly as a butterfly
She is green like a bush
She is as big as an elephant
She is odd like a bat
She is Princess Fiona.

Aisling McMenemy (7)
St Joseph's RC Primary School, Aberdeen

My First Riddle - Little Riddlers

Cheryl Cole

She is pretty like a flower,
She has red hair like a rose,
She is as happy as a princess,
She is as tall as a tree,
She is a singer like an angel,
She is kind like my teacher,
She is Cheryl Cole.

Deidra Dias Alberto (5)
St Joseph's RC Primary School, Aberdeen

Hello Kitty

She is cute like a butterfly,
She is little like a ladybird,
She is pretty like a love heart,
She is soft like a teddy bear,
She is friendly like a bee,
She is Hello Kitty.

Leah McAllister (6)
St Joseph's RC Primary School, Aberdeen

Steve Backshall

He is as cool as a cat,
He is as brave as a lion,
He is as funny as a clown,
He is amazing like a wizard,
He is Steve Backshall from 'Live and Deadly'.

Cian Mair (6)
St Joseph's RC Primary School, Aberdeen

Millie

She is as curly as spaghetti,
She is as pretty as confetti,
She is young like a kitten,
She is cuddly like a mitten,
She is as nice as a lily,
She is my sister, Millie.

Ben Scott (5)
St Joseph's RC Primary School, Aberdeen

My Dad

He is as loud as a coyote,
He is as big as a bear,
He is as chatty as Mister Chatterbox,
He is as cuddly as a puppy,
He is my dad.

Tyler Kelly (6)
St Matthew's RC Primary School, Jarrow

Alice Kenedy

She has hair as brown as chocolate
She has blue eyes.
She has ears as big as a pedal.
She has a nose as small as a pebble.

Sophie Grimes (6)
St Matthew's RC Primary School, Jarrow

He Is My Dad

He is as fun as a fair.
He is as tall as a giraffe.
He is as mint as everything.
I love him because he takes me everywhere around the world.
He is so nice to me.
He is my dad.

Daniel Stark (6)
St Matthew's RC Primary School, Jarrow

My Guinea Pig, Donna

She is as loud as a gorilla.
She is as pretty as a puffball.
She is like a feather.
She is my guinea pig, Donna.

Alexandra McLeod (6)
St Matthew's RC Primary School, Jarrow

He Is My Dad

He is as friendly as a flower.
He is as nice as a love heart.
He is as cheeky as a gorilla.
He is as beautiful as the sun.
He is as big as a gate.
He loves me very much.

Emily Bateman (6)
St Matthew's RC Primary School, Jarrow

He Is My Daddy

He is as tall as a tree.
His eyes are as blue as the sky.
He is as funny as a bunny.
He is as fast as a car.
He is as tickly as my toes.

Alex James Currie (7)
St Matthew's RC Primary School, Jarrow

She Is My Sister

She is as fast as a cheetah
She is as tall as her friend
Her hair is as brown as chocolate
Her braces are as blue as a blue whale
She is my sister, Lauren.

Tom Paterson (6)
St Matthew's RC Primary School, Jarrow

She Is Fluffy, My Hamster

She is as loud as a monkey saying, 'Oo aa.'
She is as cheeky as a monkey.
Her eyes are as black as gorilla's fur.
She is as greedy as a goat.
She is as pretty as a flower.

Libby Robertson (6)
St Matthew's RC Primary School, Jarrow

My Cousin, Rona

She has brown eyes just like chocolate.
She is two years old.
She is a tinker like a robber.
She is smart like a bird.
She has brown hair like a kitten.
She is my cousin, Rona.

Erin Bryce (6)
St Matthew's RC Primary School, Jarrow

My Dad

He is as funny as a clown.
He is as tall as a tree.
He is my dad.

Jack Thomas Gibson (5)
St Matthew's RC Primary School, Jarrow

My Dad

He is as nice as my cousin.
He is as playful as my grandma.
He is as fat as a pig.
He is as funny as a clown.
He has got short hair like my grandad.
He is as loud as a trumpet.
He is my dad.

Harry Birrell (5)
St Matthew's RC Primary School, Jarrow

My Nana

She is as funny as a clown.
She is as nice as my dad.
She has blonde hair like the sun.
She is my nana.

Cain Harry Conner (5)
St Matthew's RC Primary School, Jarrow

My First Riddle - Little Riddlers

My Mam

She is as funny as a clown.
She has blue eyes like the sky.
She is as tall as a teen.
She is my mam.

Matthew Sproston (5)
St Matthew's RC Primary School, Jarrow

My Mam

She is as funny as a clown.
She is as playful as a mouse.
She is as kind as a heart.
She is my mam.

Thomas Booth & Jay Robinson (5)
St Matthew's RC Primary School, Jarrow

What Am I?

I am green
I am round
I am crunchy
You can eat me
An apple.

Niamh Sharkey (5)
St Ninian's Primary School, Dedridge

What Am I?

I am round
I am orange
I glow up in the dark
I am scary
A pumpkin.

Chrissy Annal (6)
St Ninian's Primary School, Dedridge

My First Riddle - Little Riddlers

What Am I?

I have got a cat.
I have a black hat.
I have black hair.
I play on a broomstick.
A witch.

Alan B Shibu (6)
St Ninian's Primary School, Dedridge

What Am I?

I am orange.
I am scary.
I am round.
I glow in the dark.
A pumpkin.

Jodie Lee Scott (6)
St Ninian's Primary School, Dedridge

What Am I?

I say, 'Woo.'
I come out at night.
If you touch me I will go right through you
I say, 'Boo.'

A ghost.

Taylor Green (6)
St Ninian's Primary School, Dedridge

The Strongest Footballer

He is as furry as an ape.
He is as fast as a rocket.
He is as strong as a gorilla.
He is as cheeky as a monkey.
He is David Silva.

Daniel Strickland (7)
St Ninian's Primary School, Dedridge

A Brilliant Footballer

He is faster than light
He is as smiley as a clown
He is the bravest one I know
He is good at control
He is Kaka, from Brazil.

Andrew Robertson (7)
St Ninian's Primary School, Dedridge

My Best Friend

She is as jolly as a clown.
She is as friendly as a queen.
She is as nice as a cat.
She is as cuddly as a dog.
She is as pretty as my mum.
She is my best friend, Meghan.

Katie Meldrum
St Ninian's Primary School, Dedridge

The White Polar Bear

She is as white as a polar bear
She is as cheeky as a monkey
She is as beautiful as a pop star
She is as kind as Santa Claus
She is as cuddly as a teddy bear
She is my sister, Kim.

Katie Coyle (7)
St Ninian's Primary School, Dedridge

The Little Girl

She is as cute as a dog
She is as jolly as a clown
She is as pretty as a cat
She is as cheeky as a monkey
She is as helpful as Dad
She is Katie, my friend.

Meghan McVey (7)
St Ninian's Primary School, Dedridge

My First Riddle - Little Riddlers

My Pet

He is as black as night.
He is as brave as me.
He is as jolly as a clown.
He is as handsome as a prince.
He is as cute as a cat.
He is as cuddly as a teddy bear.
He is as cheeky as a monkey.
He is as friendly as my friend.
He is as helpful as my dad.
He is my dog, Jack.

Roha Ajmal (7)
St Ninian's Primary School, Dedridge

A Brilliant Footballer

He is as fast as a train.
He is as strong as a wrestler.
He is as brave as me.
He is as jolly as a clown.
He is John Terry.

Euan Scott (6)
St Ninian's Primary School, Dedridge

My Best Cousin

She is as cute as a mouse
She is as jolly as a clown
She is as strong as Josh
She is as cheeky as a monkey
She is as kind as Santa Claus
She is as beautiful as a princess
She is as friendly as Cameron
She is Ruby, my cousin.

Dylan Polland
St Ninian's Primary School, Dedridge

My Best Friend

He is as kind as a clown
He is as fast as a cheetah
He is as cool as a giant
He is as funny as a clown
He is Keiren, my best friend,

Aaron Duddridge (7)
St Ninian's Primary School, Dedridge

Four-Armed Friend

He is as fast as a cheetah
He is as brave as me
He is as cool as John
He is as small as an ant
He is Oscar, my puppy.

Daniel Miller (7)
St Ninian's Primary School, Dedridge

Mummy

She cooks like a chef.
She is as sweet as a lily.
She is as perfect as anything.
Her eyes are as brown as chocolate.
She is as helpful as a teacher.
She is my mum!

Aliya Iqbal
St Ninian's Primary School, Dedridge

My Mummy

She is as warm as warm.
She smells like a rose.
She gives you lots of kisses.
She is as lovely as a flower.
She works as a doctor.
She is as beautiful as snow.
She has long, beautiful, mousey hair.
Her eyes are as nice as silver.
She is my mummy!

Katherine Robertson (7)
St Ninian's Primary School, Dedridge

My Pet

She is as soft as a teddy bear
She is as small as a mouse
She is as black as the night sky
She is as ginger as a ginger cat
She is as white as snow
She climbs like a monkey
Who is she?
She's my kitten.

Lucy Neilson
St Ninian's Primary School, Dedridge

My First Riddle – Little Riddlers

My Little Sister

She is as tiny as a mouse.
She kicks like my cousin.
I listen to my mum's belly.
And I hear her heart beat.
It goes like *boom, boom, boom*.
She is going to be called Lilly.

Rachael McMaster
St Ninian's Primary School, Dedridge

Mummy

She is as good as a butterfly.
She cooks like a chef.
She smells like a rose.
She is as lovely as ever.
She is as beautiful as a rose.
She loves me as much.
She is so lovely.
I love my mummy.
She is as funny as a mouse.
She laughs like an elephant.
She buys me things.
She is lovely, really lovely.
She is cuddly like a teddy bear.

Aimee White
St Ninian's Primary School, Dedridge

My Dad

He is as strong as a rhino.
He is as handsome as can be.
He cooks like a chef.
He cares like a teacher.
He reads the best stories.
That's right! He's my daddy!

Emma Thomson
St Ninian's Primary School, Dedridge

Bird Called Spike

He is as soft as a feather.
He is as cute as a bunny.
He has a tail as big as an elephant.
He is as noisy as an alarm clock.
He is as small as a mouse.
He eats like a monster.
He is as slow as a snail.
He has eyes as cute as a rose.
He flies like a butterfly.
He bites like a dog.
He is like a big monster.
He has a beak like teeth.
He sneezes very cutely like a mouse.
He is as yellow as the sun.
He is my bird.

Amy Wood (7)
St Ninian's Primary School, Dedridge

Hannah Montana

She is a singer like me,
She is cool like an ice lolly,
She is awesome like a rock star,
She is cute like a girl,
She is Hannah Montana.

Ioan Borromeo (5)
St Robert's RC Primary School, Bridgend

Torres

He is strong like a football player,
He is smart like a rock star,
He is the best player,
He is as fast as a leopard,
He is Torres.

Osian Howell-Doyle (5)
St Robert's RC Primary School, Bridgend

Hannah Montana

She is beautiful like a rose
She is lovely like a pretty girl
She is wonderful
I like her
She is Hannah Montana.

Yasmine Evans (5)
St Robert's RC Primary School, Bridgend

The Stig

He is famous like a rock star,
He is clever like a tiger,
He is fast like a cheetah,
He drives like a racing driver,
He is Stig.

George Hunt (5)
St Robert's RC Primary School, Bridgend

My First Riddle - Little Riddlers

Grandma

She is a good person like a smiley face,
She is cool like a rock star,
She is lovely like a flower,
She is my grandma.

Ewan Bailey (5)
St Robert's RC Primary School, Bridgend

Michael Jackson

He is nice.
He is lovely like an owl.
He sings like a pop star.
He is like a sky.
He is handsome like my dad.
He is smooth like a wall.
He is lovely like a book.
He is Michael Jackson, a pop star.

Jake Stocks (5)
St Robert's RC Primary School, Bridgend

A Tiger

He is an animal like a lion
He is cute like a star
He is endangered like a polar bear
He is a tiger - *roar.*

Emily Lloyd (6)
St Robert's RC Primary School, Bridgend

He Is Jason Derulo

He is cool like a pigeon
He is nice like a book
He sings like a bird
He is trendy
He is Jason Derulo.

Elis James (6)
St Robert's RC Primary School, Bridgend

My First Riddle - Little Riddlers

Bhutan

He is dangerous like a dragon
He is fast like a leopard
He is sharp like glass
He is soft like a teddy
He is Bhutan our class tiger friend.

Amelia Rees (6)
St Robert's RC Primary School, Bridgend

Shane Williams

He is little like a mouse
He is fast like a rat
He is cool like a book
He is nice like a bunny
He is a high jumper
He is Shane Williams
A rugby player.

Elis Major (6)
St Robert's RC Primary School, Bridgend

Mrs Hopes

She is as cool as a cat
She is fun like a dog
She is as funny as a flower
She is as cool as a panda
She is as fabulous as a puppy
She is as silly as a castle
She is Mrs Hopes, our school dinner lady.

Sophie Hunter (7)
St Robert's RC Primary School, Bridgend

Niamh

She is like a cat
She is like a flower
She is like a panda
She is like a puppy
She is like a rabbit
She is like a queen
She is like a snake
She is like a castle
She is like a friend
She is Niamh.

Zoe Thomas (6)
St Robert's RC Primary School, Bridgend

Rock Star

He is cool like a rock star,
He is nice like a robin,
He is lovely like a Husky,
He is great like a Bull Terrier,
He is special like a present,
He is Michael Jackson.

Cavan Frowen (6)
St Robert's RC Primary School, Bridgend

My Teacher

She is cool like a cat,
She is like a pretty flower,
She is like a panda bear,
She is like a puppy,
She is like a queen,
She is Mrs Horn
My favourite teacher.

Kitty Long (6)
St Robert's RC Primary School, Bridgend

My Special Friend, Santa

He is cool like a rock star
He is kind like a hamster
He is lovely like a flower
He is important like the king
He is Santa Claus.

Evan Gregory (6)
St Robert's RC Primary School, Bridgend

Jason Derulo

He is a singer like Michael Jackson
He is good like a dog
He is cool like a dolphin
He is good like a horse
He is clever like a cat
He is handsome like a bull
He is nice like a magpie
He is awesome like a teacher
He is Jason Derulo.

Orlando Diogo (7)
St Robert's RC Primary School, Bridgend

My First Riddle - Little Riddlers

Ruby

She is sweet like a strawberry
She is pretty like a flower
She is like a rose
She is cute like a kitten
She is lovely
She is Ruby, my friend.

Niamh Harris (6)
St Robert's RC Primary School, Bridgend

Cheetah

It is a great eater,
It is wild like a clown,
It is dangerous like a wasp,
It is a good tracker like a tiger,
It is a cheetah.

Ruben Morgan (7)
St Robert's RC Primary School, Bridgend

Cheetah

It is fast like a Ferrari
It is nasty like a crocodile
It is dangerous like a wasp
It roars loud like a cheetah
It is horrible like a gorilla
It is as nasty as a tiger
It is as nasty as a snake
It is a cheetah.

Davide Belsole (6)
St Robert's RC Primary School, Bridgend

Cheetah

It is big like an elephant
It climbs like a monkey
It is a meat eater like a tiger
It is sharp like a knife
It is a cheetah.

Chloe Protheroe (6)
St Robert's RC Primary School, Bridgend

My First Riddle - Little Riddlers

African Hunting Dog

It is dangerous like a king cobra
It is as strong as a tiger
It is as cute as a kitten
It is as wild as a cheetah
It is clever like my brother
It is awesome like a dog
It is an African hunting dog.

Owen Stone (6)
St Robert's RC Primary School, Bridgend

Elmer

It has four legs
It comes from Africa
It is multicoloured and has got a trunk and big ears
What is it?
It is Elmer the elephant.

Talisha Cooper (7)
South Wootton First School, South Wootton

Colourful Days

He has a long tail and wants to be grey every day.
He has different colours.
He has pink, purple, red, yellow, green, blue,
orange, brown, white, black and grey.
He is funny.
He has a trunk and big ears.

What is he?

He is Elmer the elephant.

Olivia Sharp (7)
South Wootton First School, South Wootton

Rats!

I have sharp claws and I am naughty.
I nibble people's ankles and I am vicious.
I sneak in towns, I am sneaky too.
I carry germs.
What am I?
I am a rat!

Caitlin McCallum (6)
South Wootton First School, South Wootton

My First Riddle - Little Riddlers

Robin Hood

I am a brave and clever man
I have a bow and arrows
I give people help
I hide in trees.

I am Robin Hood.

Cameron Reed (7)
South Wootton First School, South Wootton

Who Am I?

I am a pretty princess
I like going to the ball
I like wearing pink clothes
My favourite colour is gold
I am friendly
I am Aurora.

Sophie Moyse (6)
South Wootton First School, South Wootton

Who Am I?

I am a boy
I save people
I am a hero
I like Supergirl
I am super strong
Who am I?
I am Superman.

Harry Ponting (6)
South Wootton First School, South Wootton

Harry Potter

I am magic
I am fast on my broomstick
I have a magic wand
I have a flying broomstick
I am powerful and I go to school at Hogwarts
Who am I?
Harry Potter.

Brad Denham (6)
South Wootton First School, South Wootton

My First Riddle – Little Riddlers

Rats!

They are vicious and nibble things.
They carry lots of germs.
They have sharp teeth.
They have a pink tail and ears.
What are they?
Rats!

Tayah Farnham (7)
South Wootton First School, South Wootton

Who Am I?

He is mean, he is horrid as well
He is scary and has fleas
He comes from Little Red Riding Hood and
The three little pigs too

Who is he?

The wolf.

Chloe McGiven (7)
South Wootton First School, South Wootton

Rats!

I am furry
I like to nibble things
I am mean
I have four legs and whiskers
I am a rat.

Emily Cullen (6)
South Wootton First School, South Wootton

The Princess

I am kind
I have a lovely dress
I am beautiful
I am sparkly
I don't hurt anyone
I wear a tiara
Who am I?
A princess.

Sophie Morgan (7)
South Wootton First School, South Wootton

My First Riddle - Little Riddlers

Who Am I?

I am nice to love and I am fantastic
I am nice to meet
I am good at things
I am small but grumpy
I am friends with Snow White
Who am I?
Grumpy.

Callum Eke (6)
South Wootton First School, South Wootton

Untitled

He likes football,
He is fast like lightning,
He is Wayne Rooney.

Cody Sharratt (6)
Stanley Grove School, Wakefield

Mum

She is beautiful
She lets me play outside
She is my mum.

Michael Blick (6)
Stanley Grove School, Wakefield

My Mummy

She's as bright as a star
She's as happy as a monkey
She's as sweet as a teddy bear
She's as funny as a monkey
She is my mum.

Hollie Smith (6)
Stanley Grove School, Wakefield

Untitled

She lets me play with my kitten.
She helps me tidy my bedroom.
She is my mum.

Amelia Ashton (5)
Stanley Grove School, Wakefield

What Furry Animal?

He is as fast as a cheetah
He has sharp teeth like a bear
He can climb trees
He is a leopard.

Mason Nunn (6)
Stanley Grove School, Wakefield

Untitled

He is as fast as a kangaroo,
He dances like a clown,
He is as fat as a clown,
He is Jack.

Ellie Wilkinson (6)
Stanley Grove School, Wakefield

My Sister

She dances like a ballerina,
She is as lazy as a hippo,
She is as kind as a sweetheart,
She is Phoebe, my sister.

Caris Riley (6)
Stanley Grove School, Wakefield

Untitled

She is like a mouse
She is like a snake
She is like a lion
She is as happy as a cat
She is like a leopard
She is like a ray of sunshine
She is Mayesi, my cousin.

Amy Whyte (6)
Stanley Grove School, Wakefield

My Friend

She is as pretty as a flower,
She is as cheeky as a monkey,
She likes to laugh,
She is my friend, Katie.

Alice Aveyard (5)
Stanley Grove School, Wakefield

Untitled

She looks like a princess,
She is cuddlier than a cat,
She is fast like a gorilla,
She is Amy, my friend.

Abigail Cooney (6)
Stanley Grove School, Wakefield

Grandpa

He is as lazy as a gorilla,
He is as lazy as a frog,
He is my grandpa.

Joseph Berry (6)
Stanley Grove School, Wakefield

My First Riddle - Little Riddlers

My Cousin, Evie

She is as cute as a flower,
She is as sweet as honey,
She is as cool as a singer,
She is as cheeky as a monkey,
She is as helpful as my mum,
She is as wonderful as a rainbow,
She is as cuddly as a teddy bear,
She is as cute as a cat,
Her eyes are like diamonds,
She is my cousin, Evie.

Georgina Odgers (6)
Stanley Grove School, Wakefield

Untitled

He is as funny as a clown,
He is as fast as rollerskates,
He is as cool as a disco,
He is as helpful as a bear,
He is Lucas.

Katie Whyte (6)
Stanley Grove School, Wakefield

My Friend

She is as funny as a cheeky monkey on a tree,
She is as beautiful as a pony,
She is as clever as a bouncing frog,
She is as helpful as a kangaroo,
She is Mayesi, my friend.

Ella Crispin (6)
Stanley Grove School, Wakefield

Untitled

She plays teachers,
She plays in my bedroom,
She tidies my bedroom with me,
She is my sister, Jessica.

Paige Wright (5)
Stanley Grove School, Wakefield

My First Riddle - Little Riddlers

The Funny Monkey Of The Jungle

It's as hairy as a lion
It's as funny as a clown
It swings like an acrobat
It's as cheeky as my brother Daniel
It's as jumpy as a kangaroo
It's as brown as mud

It's a monkey!

John Campbell (6)
Star Of The Sea RC Primary School, Whitley Bay

He's...

He's as fluffy as a pom-pom
He's as cute as a polar bear
He's as cuddly as a teddy bear
He's as white as snow
He's as old as the hills
He's a Dougal dog.

Molly Dutton (6)
Star Of The Sea RC Primary School, Whitley Bay

Bananas

He has a tail, long and curled, like a cat,
He's got fur, as soft as a kitten,
He is brown and nice, like chocolate,
He is cheeky, but cuddly,
He is Bananas, my toy monkey.

James May (6)
Star Of The Sea RC Primary School, Whitley Bay

Killer The Fish

He is as little as a pea,
He is as thin as a bone,
He is as swimmy as a dolphin,
He is as golden as treasure,
He is as quiet as a mouse,
He is as slimy as a slug,
He's my fish, Killer!

Kian MacOscar (6)
Star Of The Sea RC Primary School, Whitley Bay

My First Riddle - Little Riddlers

What Is It?

It's as cute as can be
It's as cuddly as a soft toy
It's as white as snow
It's as black as charcoal
It eats bamboo
It can live in a zoo

It's a panda.

Isabel Hines (6)
Star Of The Sea RC Primary School, Whitley Bay

I Love my Mum

She is as beautiful as flowers
She shines as bright as the sun
She cleans better than a Hoover
She is more amazing than race cars
She cooks better than my dad
She is my mum.

Barbod Farokhzad (7)
Star Of The Sea RC Primary School, Whitley Bay

He Is . . .

He is as friendly as the BFG
He is as gentle as Shrek
He is as handsome as Prince Charming
He is as caring as the dwarves
He is as kind as the genie
He is as clever as Jack
He is as cuddly as the bears
He is as big as the giant
He is *my dad!*

I love my dad.

Jonny Worrall (6)
Star Of The Sea RC Primary School, Whitley Bay

She Is Who?

She is sometimes funny.
She is sometimes cross.
She is sometimes busy.
She is sometimes dizzy.
She is sometimes my best friend.
She is always there.
She is my mum.

Chrysta Lois (6)
Star Of The Sea RC Primary School, Whitley Bay

My First Riddle - Little Riddlers

My Sister

She is as dribbly as a striker
She is as cute as a lion cub
She is as yummy as my mummy
She is as splashy in the bath as a fishy in a dishy
She's a very special missy
She's my lovely little sissy
Olivia Rose.

Amelia Slaven (6)
Star Of The Sea RC Primary School, Whitley Bay

My Cute Little Buddy!

She has big blue eyes and a cute little smile.
She has curly blonde hair,
Try to comb it if you dare!
She's a very good girl especially when she's with me!
That is why I like her to come to my house for tea.
She likes to play with my toys and make lots of noise
She's a cute little princess
As sweet as can be
She's my baby cousin, Sarah.

Chloe-Marie Davison (6)
Star Of The Sea RC Primary School, Whitley Bay

A Special Girl

She's as naughty as a chimp
She's as pretty as a pony
She's as cheeky as a monkey
She's as small as a kitten
She's as cuddly as a teddy
She's my little sister, Iris.

Gabriel Darcy (6)
Star Of The Sea RC Primary School, Whitley Bay

My Labrador - Wispa

Her coat is black and shiny
Her nose is cold and wet
She barks as loud as thunder
My Wispa I will never forget.

Amy Tullock (6)
Star Of The Sea RC Primary School, Whitley Bay

Little Angel

She is as little as a ladybird
She is as smooth as snow
She wriggles like a worm
She crawls like a crab
She cries like a cat
She sleeps like a sheep
She is Rose, my little sister.

Joseph Mathew (7)
Star Of The Sea RC Primary School, Whitley Bay

Twiddly Riddle

I'm as cute as a kitten,
I'm as small as a mouse,
I'm as fluffy as a duckling,
I can jump like a kangaroo from tree to tree,
I snatch bananas from branches,
Because I'm a marmoset.

Bella Gott (7)
Star Of The Sea RC Primary School, Whitley Bay

Brian

He can run very fast,
Although he's getting fat,
He is sweet when he squeaks,
When he jumps it's funny,
But he is *not* a bunny!
He is my guinea pig.

Abigail Stephenson (6)
Star Of The Sea RC Primary School, Whitley Bay

The Chameleon

It is a lizard,
It has big googly eyes,
It changes colour,
To camouflage and hide,
It has a long tongue like a frog,
It's a chameleon.

Dominic Dixon (7)
Star Of The Sea RC Primary School, Whitley Bay

My First Riddle - Little Riddlers

Who Is She?

She's as cute as a newborn baby
She's as naughty as my brother
She's as black as night
She's as cuddly as a teddy bear
She's as hungry as a giant
She's as friendly as me
She's my cousin's lovely dog, Bonnie.

Martha Foreman (7)
Star Of The Sea RC Primary School, Whitley Bay

My Pet

It is fluffy as cotton wool.
It has claws and teeth as sharp as a needle.
Its eyes are shiny as diamonds.
It is soft as a cushion and sleeps all day.
It is a cat.

Josephine Perella (6)
Star Of The Sea RC Primary School, Whitley Bay

Untitled

He is as naughty as a dragon
He is as funny as a clown
He is as fast as a cheetah
He is as fluffy as a teddy bear
He is as greedy as a pig
He is as cheeky as a monkey
He is as white as a cloud
He is my rabbit, Snowy.

Drew Lake (6)
Tanfield Lea Primary School, Stanley

Baby Brothers

He is as cute as a bunny
He is as evil as the Devil
He is a fierce dinosaur
He is as naughty as a cheeky monkey
He is as clever as a clown
He is littler than a mouse
He is as strong as an ox
He is my brother, Jaidon.

Anais Little (7)
Tanfield Lea Primary School, Stanley

My First Riddle - Little Riddlers

He Is . . .

He is as boring as a yo-yo.
He's as cool as a tomboy.
He is as beautiful as a poppy.
He is as funny as a silly clown.
He is as soft as a bed cover.
He is as cuddly as a fuzzy bunny.
He is Teeky, my cat.

Tia Bailey (7)
Tanfield Lea Primary School, Stanley

To Gran Maisie

She is as little as a kitten.
She is as nice as a flower.
She is as smooth as a cloud.
She is as lovely as a tart.
She is as clever as sunshine.
She is as cool as a cat.
She is as furry as a dog.
She is as silly as a goat.
She is my hamster.

Elle Stark (6)
Tanfield Lea Primary School, Stanley

My Dad

He is as cuddly as a dog.
He is as fluffy as a rabbit.
He is as angry as a grizzly bear.
He is as fussy as a kid.
He is as smelly as a pig.
He is as slimy as a slug.

Jamie Miley (6)
Tanfield Lea Primary School, Stanley

My Friend, Sasha

She is as nice as a flower.
She is as kind as a dog.
She is as slow as a tortoise.
She is as cool as a pop star.
She is as beautiful as the countryside.
She is as funny as a doctor.
She is my friend, Sasha.

Beth Nash (6)
Tanfield Lea Primary School, Stanley

My First Riddle - Little Riddlers

My Pet Fish, Sophie

She is as stripy as a tiger.
She is as cool as a rock star.
She is as clever as a gymnast.
She is as naughty as a child.
She is as cool as a cat.
She is as greedy as a pig.
She is as beautiful as a flower.
She is my fish, Sophie.

Lauren Urquhart-Arnold (6)
Tanfield Lea Primary School, Stanley

Dad

He is as soft as a tiger
He is as cuddly as a teddy
He is as strong as an elephant
He is as good as a golfer
He is my dad.

Aron Alderson (6)
Tanfield Lea Primary School, Stanley

Mum

She is as beautiful as a flower
She is as sweet as sugar
She is as lovely as a peach
She is my wonderful mum.

Allana Alderson (6)
Tanfield Lea Primary School, Stanley

The Pop Star

She is cool like an ice cream
She is as pretty as a picture
She is as beautiful as a flower
She is a pop star
She is Hannah Montana.

Rebecca Bell (6)
Tanfield Lea Primary School, Stanley

My First Riddle - Little Riddlers

My Teacher, Mrs Brown

She is as kind as a daisy
She is as beautiful as a flower
She is as friendly as a cat
She is as sweet as a girl
She is my teacher, Mrs Brown.

Ben Henley (6)
Tanfield Lea Primary School, Stanley

Untitled

She is as crazy as a pig
She is as funny as a clown
She is as cool as an ice lolly
She is as nice as a flower
She is my friend, Brooke.

Joe Little (6)
Tanfield Lea Primary School, Stanley

My Cat, Bonny!

She is as beautiful as a flower
She is as cool as a pop star
She is as cute as a kitten
She's as clever as a clown
She's as hungry as a goat
She's as playful as a puppy
She's as stripy as a tiger
She's as cuddly as a teddy bear
She's my cat, Bonny.

Tamzin McAdam (7)
Tanfield Lea Primary School, Stanley

My Dog, Henry

He is as fussy as a cat.
He is as funny as a clown.
He is as whiffy as an elephant.
He is as horrid as Henry.
He is as sweet as a dog.
He is as shiny as the sun.
He is my dog and he is fun.

Sophie Steel (6)
Tanfield Lea Primary School, Stanley

My First Riddle - Little Riddlers

My Puppy

He is as quiet as a ladybird
He is as jumpy as a grasshopper
He is as naughty as a fox
He is as dirty as a sheep
He is my puppy.

James Collinge (5)
Tundergarth Primary School, Lockerbie

My Gran's Kitten

He is quieter than Santa Claus
He is better than the world
He is cuter than a lion
He is naughtier than a dog
He is blacker than coal
Who is he?
He's my gran's kitten.

Kelly Halliday (6)
Tundergarth Primary School, Lockerbie

Lion

Big as a dinosaur
Clean as soap
Noisy as a dog
Big ears.

Sandy Temple (5)
Tundergarth Primary School, Lockerbie

Sparkle

He jumps up on me
He is smelly
He is naughty
He likes me
He is wild
He bites
He eats chewing gum!

Dari Earl (5)
Tundergarth Primary School, Lockerbie

My First Riddle - Little Riddlers

Young Writers Information

We hope you have enjoyed reading this book - and that you will continue to enjoy it in the coming years.
If you like reading and writing poetry drop us a line, or give us a call, and we'll send you a free information pack.
Alternatively if you would like to order further copies of this book or any of our other titles, then please give us a call or log onto our website at www.youngwriters.co.uk.

Young Writers Information
Remus House
Coltsfoot Drive
Peterborough
PE2 9BF
(01733) 890066